TWISTED JOURNEYS #6

THE TIME TRAVEL TRAP

DAN JOLLEY

ILLUSTRATED BY MATT WENDT

LERNER BOOKS · LONDON · NEW YORK · MINNEAPOLIS

Story by Dan Jolley

Pencils and inks by Matt Wendt

Colouring by Hi-Fi Design

Lettering by Marshall Dillon & Terri Delgado

Graphic Universe™ is a trademark and Twisted Journeys® is a registered trademark of Lerner Publishing Group, Inc.

First published in the United Kingdom in 2009 by
Lerner Books,
Dalton House,
60 Windsor Avenue,
London SW19 2RR

Website address: www.lernerbooks.co.uk

This edition was updated and edited for UK publication by Discovery Books Ltd.,
First Floor, 2 College Street, Ludlow, Shropshire SY8 1AN

British Library Cataloguing in Publication Data

Jolley, Dan
 The time travel trap. - 2nd ed. - (Twisted journeys)
 1. Time travel - Comic books, strips, etc. - Juvenile
 fiction 2. Plot-your-own stories 3. Children's stories -
 Comic books, strips, etc.
 I. Title
 741.5

ISBN-13: 978 0 7613 4413 1

Printed in Singapore

It's the annual science competition!

Children from all over the county are here to compete. The school sports hall is packed, table after table. There must be two hundred entrants. You know you'll beat them all though. Your experiment on the mating habits of earthworms is guaranteed to win. At least you think it is until you see who comes in and sets up right next to you.

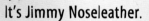

It's Jimmy Noseleather.

You can't help but groan. Jimmy's father is the world-famous scientist Dr Felix Noseleather, and if he helped Jimmy with his project, you might be sunk.

Jimmy sets a high-tech-looking device on the table. Argh!

'Hey, Jimmy,' you ask, 'did your dad give you a hand with that?'

'Sort of,' Jimmy replies. 'I snuck a few of his plans out of his office and built it myself.'

'No kidding? Huh. You, uh . . . you sure that was a good idea?'

GO ON TO THE NEXT PAGE.

With a huge flash of light, Jimmy's machine creates a sort of portal. It just hangs there in mid-air in front of you. You hear people screaming and running, but you're fascinated.

The doorway is sort of like a TV screen. You can see another place through it — a place with green grass. A horse trots by . . . and then the scene changes.

Now you're looking at a rocky hillside. The trees and plants look strange. You can't decide exactly how they look strange, but they do. The scene changes back and then back and forth, back and forth.

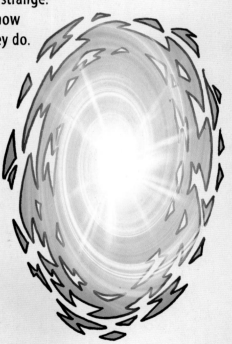

That's when you realize the doorway is pulling you towards it!

You try to break free, but you can't. You're going through, like it or not.

GO ON TO THE NEXT PAGE.

What you can see through the doorway keeps switching as you're pulled towards the door.

WILL YOU . . .

. . . aim for the grassy place where you saw the horse?

TURN TO PAGE 18.

. . . go for the rocky hillside with the weird plants?

TURN TO PAGE 106.

Everyone here is scared to death of this guy! And if you stick around, you'll end up just like them.

WILL YOU . . .

. . . look out for yourself and make a dash for the doorway alone?
TURN TO PAGE 85.

. . . convince them to revolt and lead them through the doorway?
TURN TO PAGE 69.

'How am I supposed to know where you are?' you say loudly. 'I don't even know where I am!'

As you watch, the point of light transforms into a hideous alien creature! It's sort of like a huge, slimy green beanbag, except it's almost all mouth. Two beady little eyes pop open above the huge mouth. Then the mouth smiles, and it's filled with hundreds of spiny teeth.

'That sounded very rude,' the alien says. 'There was no need to be so impolite.'

'I, uh, didn't mean to sound rude.' You slowly back away from it and head towards the door.

'We treat rude children in a very decisive manner,' it says.

Stalling for time, you ask, 'Um — what exactly do you do to them?'

The creature begins rolling towards you. 'We eat them!' it screams.

The huge tooth-filled mouth opens wide and as its foul breath washes over you, you realize that this is

THE END

That doorway is your one chance to get home. You take a deep breath and dive under.

The water stings your eyes, but you glance over to one side — and see something out of a nightmare swimming straight towards you! It's sort of like a crocodile, but it's huge, the size of a bus!

You swim faster and faster, but its jaws are starting to open. It's got teeth the size of skateboards. It gets closer and closer and you know it could swallow you whole . . .

. . . and then – **CRASH!**

You land flat on your back, soaking wet, right in the middle of Becky Henderson's display on ultrasonic duck calls.

'Hey!' Becky shouts. Then you realize: you've come back seconds before Jimmy Noseleather's machine goes nuts.

'Excuse me,' you mumble to Becky as you scramble up. 'I've got to go shut down a time machine!'

THE END

You're not about to fling yourself head first somewhere without knowing where you're going. You'd better go and check out those cave dwellings first.

It doesn't take you long to get around to them. You discover a series of handholds and toeholds dug into the walls, and you climb around to the lowest terrace in no time. 'Hello?' you call out.

Immediately ten or eleven people come out at the sound of your voice. From the way they're dressed, you realize something straight away – they're all time travellers, like you! One wears cowboy clothes, another is clearly from Victorian times. . . They must have all been stranded here too.

The biggest one steps forward. Obviously he's in charge. And that makes you nervous, because this guy looks like . . . well, like a caveman. He's huge, and he's carrying a club.

'Who you?' he growls. 'What you want? Say, or I smash your skull!'

TWISTED JOURNEYS®

Oh, you don't like getting threatened one bit.

WILL YOU...

... swallow your pride, explain who
you are and try to make peace?

TURN TO PAGE 90.

... give this big lummox
some attitude right back?

TURN TO PAGE 110.

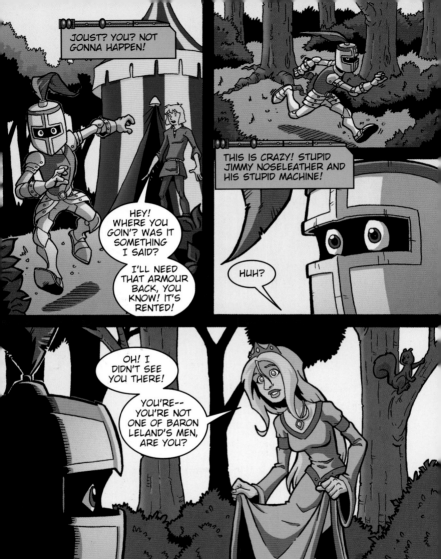

'No!' you tell her. You try to raise your visor, but it won't budge. 'I'm not from around here at all.'

The young woman takes a minute to catch her breath. 'Thank goodness! I am Princess Genevieve.'

'Princess? Uh . . . pardon me for asking, but why is a princess running alone through the woods?'

'I'm running away from Baron Leland! My father has arranged for me to marry the baron, but I do not love him! He is too old. And he smells of stinky cheese.' Her eyes light up as an idea comes to her. 'Perhaps you could help me! Clearly you are a knight. Can you aid in my escape and be my protector?'

You're about to say, 'Whoa, now, hold on,' but you don't get the chance. Suddenly men come crashing through the woods and surround you both.

GO ON TO THE NEXT PAGE.

You count a dozen soldiers, all of them wearing red and gold armour. They point deadly looking crossbows at you.

Then a short, slender, dainty man wearing fancy silk pushes past the soldiers and walks right up to you. He looks incredibly angry.

'Lord Leland!' the princess cries. 'Do not be angry with this knight! I fled alone, with help from no one!'

The baron doesn't look convinced. 'And this unknown knight just happened to encounter my bride-to-be, out here in the forest, hmmm?'

He expects an answer. You'd shrug if the armour would let you. 'Well, yeah. Basically.'

'I do not believe you! Men, take these two back to my castle! There we shall determine what is the truth and what is not!'

Back to Leland's castle? You definitely don't like the sound of that!

GO ON TO THE NEXT PAGE.

Baron Leland is a tiny man. You think you could take him — but he's got all those soldiers with him.

WILL YOU . . .

. . . challenge the baron's honour by daring him to face you in one-on-one combat?

TURN TO PAGE 31.

. . . decide to go peacefully with him and his men?

TURN TO PAGE 46.

HELP IN ENGLISH

In the blink of an eye, you're somewhere else.

The school is gone. Jimmy's gone. Jimmy's machine is gone. What just happened?

You look around.

It's like something out of a Robin Hood story.

You're on a grassy field, and all around you see brightly striped tents. People dressed in strange clothes hurry about. Some of them are leading horses and some are carrying swords.

You can hear, off to the right, the sound of galloping hooves. Then there's a loud crash and a crowd roars. It only takes you a minute to work out what's going on.

Jimmy's machine has sent you back in time. You're at a jousting tournament!

GO ON TO THE NEXT PAGE.

WHAT IF THEY CATCH YOU AND THINK YOU'RE A SPY OR SOMETHING?

YOU'D BETTER HIDE HERE UNTIL YOU CAN WORK OUT WHAT TO DO.

HELLO? ARE YOU HERE? IT'S YOUR SQUIRE.

THEY SAID I WAS TO HELP YOU GET INTO YOUR ARMOUR AND GET YOUR WEAPONS READY.

DO I HAVE THE RIGHT TENT?

THEY MIGHT KILL YOU FIRST AND ASK QUESTIONS LATER!

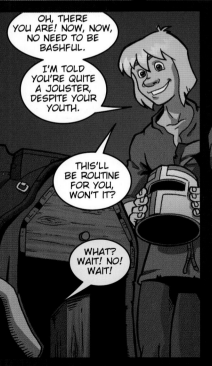

OH, THERE YOU ARE! NOW, NOW, NO NEED TO BE BASHFUL.

I'M TOLD YOU'RE QUITE A JOUSTER, DESPITE YOUR YOUTH.

THIS'LL BE ROUTINE FOR YOU, WON'T IT?

WHAT? WAIT! NO! WAIT!

YOU PROTEST, BUT THE SQUIRE DOESN'T LISTEN. AND BEFORE YOU KNOW IT ...

THERE! ALL SET!

BEST HURRY, NOW. SIR HOGARTH THE VICIOUS DOESN'T LIKE TO BE KEPT WAITING, YOU KNOW.

GO ON TO THE NEXT PAGE.

Armour? Jousting? Sir Hogarth the Vicious?
What have you got yourself into?

WILL YOU . . .

. . . play along for now and work
out how to talk your way
out of this before it's your
turn to joust?

TURN TO PAGE 54.

. . . break loose and run away, as
fast as your legs will take you?

TURN TO PAGE 14.

'Goodbye!' you shout. Leaving Princess Genevieve and the wizard behind, you rush through the doorway. In the blink of an eye, you're back at the science competition. . .

. . . where everyone is screaming! You look around and see Jimmy's machine going haywire. Huge doorways open and close at random around the room. The floor shakes as an entire herd of woolly mammoths comes thundering through.

Their trumpeting is so loud you can't hear anything else. People are running everywhere.

Somebody bangs into you and knocks you down. You look up just in time to see a huge mammoth thundering straight towards you. You won't be able to get out of the way in time, and you don't think even your suit of armour can protect you from these monsters.

'I should've stayed in the castle,' you think to yourself, just as a gigantic, woolly foot comes down right on top of you.

THE END

'I'm sorry, I don't know where you are,' you say. 'I just got here myself, actually.'

The brilliant spot of light grows dimmer, changes shape . . . and becomes a very dapper little man with silver hair, a three-piece suit and orange skin. He looks quite polite.

'So you're an unexpected visitor, then?' he asks. 'Like me — here by accident?'

'I'm afraid so. There was this incident with a broken time machine . . . Do you, um, do you know how I might get back to my own time?'

The little man pats you comfortingly on the arm. 'Perhaps, perhaps. I know how stressful it is to be thrown into an unfamiliar situation. I'm travelling from a parallel dimension, you see, and I've got myself a bit lost. But here, let's concentrate on your problem first. My technology will probably work on you.'

GO ON TO THE NEXT PAGE.

'Probably?' That's a little too uncertain for your liking. Plus, everyone was running in fear from this guy! Still, he could be your only chance.

WILL YOU...

...decide to let the alien use his technology to help you?

TURN TO PAGE 60.

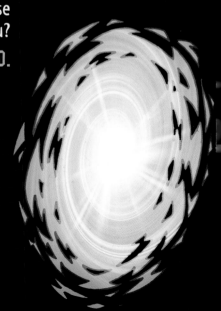

...politely tell him, 'No thanks'?

TURN TO PAGE 41.

You'd be happy to take Princess Genevieve with you! Back to modern time, the two of you go.

Luckily, you arrive unseen in an empty corner of the sports hall, behind a big potted plant.

First things first. You find the high school's metal workshop and get this stupid armour pried off.

Then you work out a way to pass Genevieve off as your older cousin from out of town. You're sure she'll fit in at school without too much trouble. One part-time job later and you've never seen anyone as happy as the former princess.

She calls you every day to thank you and tell you how much she loves it here, living life as a normal girl. That is, she calls when she's not too busy going shopping or watching television.

Normal life sounds good to you too. You promise yourself to stay far away from Jimmy Noseleather from now on.

THE END

Well, pollution or not, you can't just sit in this pod for the rest of your life. You put on the jumpsuit and the helmet. 'Hello, computer? Open door?'

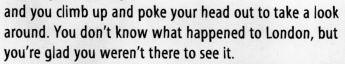

Immediately a hatch opens above you, and you climb up and poke your head out to take a look around. You don't know what happened to London, but you're glad you weren't there to see it.

The jumpsuit's kind of itchy and the helmet fogs up a little when you breathe, but it's not too bad. Maybe you can find somebody around here who can tell you what you missed — or at least how far in the future you are.

'Hello?' You call out, but you're not sure if anybody can hear you with the helmet on. 'Hello? Is anyone there?'

After a few seconds, you think you hear something off to your right. You look hard . . . and . . . yes! There in the shadows, something moved.

GO ON TO THE NEXT PAGE.

'Hello? I'm not going to hurt you!'

The thing you saw steps out of the shadows. Then another one does . . . and another . . . and another.

They're giant rats.

Except they're not exactly rats, because they're standing up on their hind legs, and they're wearing worn, tattered clothes. They're all looking at you with blood-red, intelligent eyes.

'You're not going to hurt us, huh?' the first giant rat-person says. He looks around at the others. 'The child's not going to hurt us!' The rest of the rat-people burst out laughing. The first one looks back at you. 'It's good to know you're so friendly,' he says.

'Uh . . . why do you say that?'

'Because it would be inconvenient if our lunch tried to resist!'

Then all the mutant rats swarm towards you, and you can't get back to the pod in time and this is very much

THE END

You don't know how much plant-killing juice is in that canister, but you do know you're running out of time.

WILL YOU...

...spray the plants that are chasing you?
TURN TO PAGE 39.

...throw the canister at the plants around the doorway?
TURN TO PAGE 88.

'You've got to help me!' you cry out. 'I got zapped here by mistake when a time machine went crazy! Nobody else speaks my language! I don't know what to do!'

The point of light dims and settles towards the floor. Then it turns into the ugliest alien you've ever seen or imagined. It looks sort of like a cross between a frog and a mushroom.

'Ah, so you are out of place,' it says.

'Yes! Out of place! That's right!'

The alien continues. 'You seek to join those of your own kind.'

'Well . . . yeah. Yes, I do!'

'Very good,' it says. Then it lifts a hand and a brilliant beam of light flashes out and hits you . . .

. . . and transforms you into an alien! Just like the one in front of you!

'Now you have a companion,' the alien says happily. 'And soon we will be married.'

Married?

AAAAAAAAAHHH!!

THE END

You're afraid it's too late now. Baron Leland is a master swordsman, and you . . . well, you're not. But then two things happen at exactly the same time.

First, Baron Leland's foot hits a wet patch of grass and he slips. It's a miracle! He's off balance and vulnerable, and you think you could rush in and knock him silly.

Second, you see one of Jimmy Noseleather's doorways open in the air about three metres behind the baron. Through the doorway — is that Mr Eggles the headmaster? It is! The doorway leads back to the science competition!

GO ON TO THE NEXT PAGE.

Now's your one shot!

WILL YOU...

...run around the stunned baron as fast as possible and dive through the doorway?

TURN TO PAGE 95.

...knock the baron on the head so Princess Genevieve can go free?

TURN TO PAGE 65.

HELP IN ENGLISH

GO ON TO THE NEXT PAGE.

What just happened? Everything looks funny. And . . . big. Why did the wizard make the room get bigger?

Then you realize the room's not bigger. You're smaller.

In fact, you're tiny.

You turn around to try to find a mirror, and your feet feel really strange. All four of them!

There's a mirror. You scamper over to it, and what you see nearly gives you a heart attack. The wizard turned you into a newt! How are you going to get out of this?

Then you hear the sound of soft little footsteps, and in the mirror, you see the reflection of the black cat. It's awake now and coming straight for you . . . licking its chops.

Well that's the last time you'll lie to a wizard!

THE END

It's been nine hours now . . . and you don't have any food . . . and you're not sure, but you think the escape pod's lights are getting dimmer.

Then the computer voice speaks and it sounds strange and slow. 'Pod power supply at two per cent. Shutting down in one minute, thirty seconds.'

What? 'Wait, wait, wait! Will I still have heat if you shut down?'

'Negative.'

'But it's night outside now! It's freezing! If I go now, can I make it to one of those places you showed me?'

'At current temperature, chance of success is less than one per cent. Shutting down.'

'Wait!'

Everything goes dark . . . and then the electrically sealed door pops open.

The wind that comes howling in is really cold . . . !

THE END

That lawman is most likely going to shoot first and ask questions later, and you don't want to end up full of holes.

WILL YOU ...

... drop your gun, hit the floor, cover up your head, and hope for the best?

TURN TO PAGE 91.

... point your own gun at him and tell him to calm down before someone gets hurt?

TURN TO PAGE 99.

There's no way you'll make it to the doorway with all these plants after you. You push a button on the canister, whirl around, and spray them point-blank.

The huge tendrils jerk back. They start to turn yellow and wither. You shout, 'Alright!' and head for the doorway again, but something catches your ankle.

You look down and see a fresh, green tendril coming out from underneath the ones you sprayed. It's got you, and it's not letting go. You aim at it, but the herbicide canister's empty! When you try to stamp on it with your other foot, another tendril snares that ankle too.

Plants slither across the ground and wrap around your body, pulling you off your feet. As you're dragged down into the plant mass you see the doorway shimmer and wink out of existence.

And that's the last thing you see.

THE END

You've got maybe two seconds to work out what to do before you become a bite-sized snack.

WILL YOU...

...scramble up and dive head first into the water?

TURN TO PAGE 96.

...stay perfectly still and hope the dinosaur won't see you?

TURN TO PAGE 100.

'I appreciate the offer,' you tell the alien hesitantly. 'But I'm not really comfortable trying something like that if it might not work.'

The alien shrugs. 'Not a bad choice. The process might have either turned you inside out or transformed you into a giant cucumber.' He looks around. 'So . . . I'm a little lost, and so are you. I think I'd like to explore the surrounding planets for a bit. Care to join me?'

Huh? 'You — you want me to come and fly around space with you? In your spaceship?'

'I'll have to build one out of materials from this space station, but that's only a few minutes' work. What do you say?'

'Are you joking? Tour the solar system? Absolutely!'

'Brilliant. Come with me. You can pick out colours for our vessel. By the way, my name is Nigel.'

You tell Nigel your name.

This is going to be fun.

THE END

Smoke means people, right? People might be able to help. You dig in and sprint up the hill, with the dinosaur right behind you.

It gets closer . . . you can actually feel its breath on your back! But then you spot something. There's a narrow crevice in the hillside, too small for the dinosaur to fit through. It's your only chance!

You plunge into the crevice. The walls are smeared with thick mud and leaves, and in seconds you're completely covered. But you don't care — the dinosaur can't get to you. It roars at the crevice's entrance, clawing and scraping at the earth, but you're safe.

You look around and notice something. The crevice seems to go all the way through the hill, like a narrow hallway, and it leads towards where you saw the smoke. You follow it cautiously.

42

GO ON TO THE NEXT PAGE.

You know if you stay here, there's a good chance you'll end up dead. But you don't know what's through that doorway, either!

WILL YOU...

...jump through the doorway
that has train tracks?

TURN TO PAGE 52.

...jump through the doorway that
shows the starry sky?

TURN TO PAGE 102.

...decide to head for the cliff dwellings
you saw in the valley?

TURN TO PAGE 12.

Getting to that doorway is priority number one. You charge straight for it.

The crowd cheers wildly – then boos as you veer away from Sir Hogarth.

'Coward!' someone shouts, but you truly couldn't care less about that as you dash straight through the doorway . . . and crash straight into Jimmy Noseleather's table, back at the science competition. Everyone stares as his machine flies off, hits the floor and shatters into a million pieces.

That's not what everyone's staring at though.

Everyone's staring at you, sitting on your horse in the middle of the sports hall, holding your lance and wearing a suit of armour.

'Congratulations, Jimmy,' you say nervously, raising your visor. 'Your machine works!'

Well, at least you're back in your own time, and with the armour on, it doesn't hurt when Jimmy tries to punch you for breaking his machine.

THE END

As the group moves into the castle's huge entrance hall, Princess Genevieve manages to get close enough to whisper to you.

'You've got to help me! Please, I beg you! I cannot go through with this marriage . . . and if they keep you here, you'll end up dead!'

You whisper back. 'I'd love to help you, princess, but right now, I don't really see how I can. If you think of something I could do, just let me know, all right?'

The princess looks pretty unhappy with your answer. She glances around the hall . . . and then her eyes light up with hope.

GO ON TO THE NEXT PAGE.

You follow Genevieve's line of sight and see what she reacted to. Standing over to one side, in the shadows, is an incredibly old man. He's wearing shiny purple robes and has long white hair and a long white beard that hangs down his chest. You can only think of one term to describe what he looks like: wizard.

He's watching you like a hawk, with a suspicious look on his face, but he doesn't say or do anything.

'Who is that?' you whisper to Genevieve.

She starts to answer, but Baron Leland has come up beside her and give you a menacing stare. 'Silence, you two! You shall not speak until I command you to!'

GO ON TO THE NEXT PAGE.

You decided to go with the flow before, and you're not too satisfied with the results so far. Now you're in the baron's castle, surrounded by hundreds of soldiers!

WILL YOU...

...try to get the wizard-looking old man's attention, since Genevieve seems to think he's a good guy?

TURN TO PAGE 62.

...wait till the baron gives you a chance to speak so you can finally explain everything?

TURN TO PAGE 93.

HELP IN ENGLISH

The lawman straightens up, surprised. 'What? You're a child? Here, let me help you up.'

You stand up and pull off your bandana. 'See? I'm not with these creeps! It was a case of mistaken identity. They forced me to come along.'

The lawman thinks for a moment. 'I see. You were just cooperating so they wouldn't hurt you.'

'Exactly!'

'Well, where are you from, kid? Where were you going? What were you doing all the way out here?'

That stops you for a few seconds. What do you tell him? 'Well, mister . . . I'm . . . I'm an orphan.' That's kind of true. At least until you figure out how to get back home.

'Orphaned? Hmmm. You know, I could use somebody like you — somebody who keeps cool in a tough situation. You might have a future in law enforcement, kid!'

WELL ...

IT'S NOT EXACTLY WHAT YOU HAD PLANNED FOR YOUR SUMMER HOLIDAY...

... BUT AT LEAST YOU WON'T HAVE TO DO ANY MORE HOMEWORK!

YOU READY, KID?

LET'S GO CATCH SOME BAD GUYS.

THE END

Any place is better than one filled with dinosaurs. You jump through the doorway . . .

. . . and suddenly you're in some kind of desert, all sand and cactus. You hear a train whistle in the distance and spot some railway tracks a few metres away.

'There you are!' a rough voice says. ''Bout time you showed up!'

Right behind you stands a group of four men. It hits you all at once. Cowboy hats. Six-shooters. Horses. Bandanas across the faces. They're outlaws!

You're in the American Old West!

'Better get geared up,' one of the men says. He hands you a gun belt, a hat, some gloves, and a bandana. 'I tell you whut! They don't call you the Sheboygan Kid for nothin'! You're the youngest gunslinger I ever seen!'

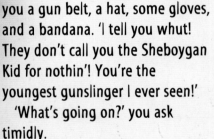

'What's going on?' you ask timidly.

'What's goin' on? We're gonna rob this train, that's what's goin' on! Now get ready!'

You're not about to rob a train! That's crazy! But these guys all have guns.

WILL YOU . . .

. . . play along for a little while and wait for the right time to escape?

TURN TO PAGE 103.

. . . try to get out of this mess immediately?

TURN TO PAGE 57.

NL 6000

You're sure you'll be able to explain the situation once you find whoever's in charge around here. So you let the squire take you outside and put you on a horse.

'Who's the boss of this place?' you ask the squire. He leads you and your horse towards the sound of the crowd.

'I beg your pardon?'

'The boss. The one in charge. The top dog. When can I talk to him or her?'

The squire grins. 'Oh, that would be Baron Leland of Tunstall.'

'Baron Leland. Good. When can I talk to him?'

'Right after your joust! He always talks to the winner. You will win, won't you?'

You'd answer him, but all of a sudden, your tongue has stuck to the roof of your mouth.

GO ON TO THE NEXT PAGE.

GO ON TO THE NEXT PAGE.

You've got to get to that doorway! But it's past Sir Hogarth the Vicious and he's itching for a fight.

WILL YOU...

... forget about all this jousting nonsense and make a break for the doorway?

TURN TO PAGE 45.

... try to surrender, so that Sir Hogarth doesn't take your head off before you can explain everything?

TURN TO PAGE 86.

... decide to face Sir Hogarth first, so he doesn't interfere when you go for the doorway?

TURN TO PAGE 22.

You're no train robber. There's got to be something you can do to foul up the outlaws' plans. You look around while you're putting on the gear the man gave you . . .

. . . and spot something in one of the guys' saddlebags. It looks like – is it? It is! It's dynamite! They must be planning to use that to blow open a safe.

What if just one stick were to go off? Say, a few dozen metres away? That would scare the horses and make them run. Plus it would tip off the people on the train that something was up.

This plan is great! All you have to do is creep over there and grab one of the sticks without anyone noticing what you're doing . . .

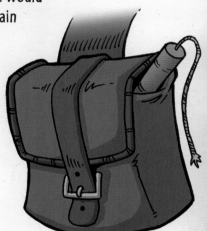

GO ON TO THE NEXT PAGE.

You move a couple of steps back and strike a match —
and at that moment, one of the outlaws turns and sees
what you're up to.

'What're you doin'?' he shouts, and just as he starts to
run towards you, the fuse lights on the stick you're holding.

All of a sudden, all the outlaws are around you. They're
grabbing and shouting, all at the same time . . .

. . . and one of them bumps your hand
hard enough that you lose your grip
on the dynamite. You
can't do anything
but watch as it tum-
bles through the
air, as if it's in
slow motion, travelling
in a perfect arc.

And it lands right in
the saddlebag with all
the other sticks of
dynamite.

Everyone freezes. The shortest
of the outlaws says, 'Well,
I bet you couldn't do that again if you tried.' And then
there's a gargantuan explosion — which means that for you,
this is

THE END

'Well, if it's no trouble.'

The alien grins. 'No trouble at all! Here, just face this direction. Oh, and here, take this. It ought to make for some good conversation.'

He hands you a small cube-shaped object. You take it hesitantly. 'Conversation? But, uh, what is – ' Before you can finish your question, the orange-skinned alien waves his hands in the air. The room gets a little wavy and distorted-looking . . .

. . . and you're back at the science competition – just like that, in the blink of an eye! You look down at the alien's device. You realize it has words engraved on the bottom:
ONE (1) MARK-7 DUST BOMB. WILL VAPORIZE ALL DUST WITHIN 50 METRES UPON ACTIVATION.

Whoa!

Forget conversation. Forget the science competition! Where's the patent office? This thing will make you rich!

THE END

You don't really want to slog through the snow, but you don't want to just sit here, either.

WILL YOU . . .

. . . stay here and try to work out how to send a distress signal?
TURN TO PAGE 36.

. . . head for the US military base? It's further away, but you know they'll speak English there.
TURN TO PAGE 74.

. . . attempt to make it to the Russian research facility? You don't speak Russian, but it's a lot closer!
TURN TO PAGE 78.

GO ON TO THE NEXT PAGE.

The baron is none too happy at the wizard's interference, but you can tell he's not about to object. 'Yes, wizard? What can I do for you?'

'I believe I shall take this prisoner off your hands,' the wizard replies calmly.

Baron Leland tries hard not to lose his temper. Finally, he gets control of himself, but his voice still trembles a little. 'Fine. All right. Guards, put the prisoner wherever the wizard says.'

'No, that won't be necessary,' the wizard says. 'I shall escort our guest myself.'

A little confused but very grateful, you go with the wizard down a narrow flight of stairs. He takes you into what looks like a magician's workshop, filled with potions and cauldrons and crystal balls. A black cat sleeps in one corner.

'Now.' He turns to you. 'Before we take that armour off, tell me exactly who you are and how you arrived here.'

GO ON TO THE NEXT PAGE.

You think this guy might have just saved your life
. . . but he's kind of scary himself!

WILL YOU . . .

. . . avoid telling him what
really happened, so he doesn't
think you're crazy?

TURN TO PAGE 34.

. . . take a chance and
explain all about the
time machine?

TURN TO PAGE 82.

You're anxious to get back home, but you really want to help Princess Genevieve get away from this scrawny little bully. He's still off balance, so you rush in and draw back your sword. One good shot with the sword's heavy handle will make him see stars, and then you can get back home with a clear conscience.

Unfortunately just as your sword arm comes down, Baron Leland throws a hand up and catches your wrist.

'You'll make a fine slave in my rock quarries,' Leland says through gritted teeth.

Then the flat of his sword thunks into the side of your helmet. The princess screams . . . and just before everything goes black, you see the doorway fade out and disappear.

Looks as if you've got a life of breaking rocks to look forward to. Still, look on the bright side. At least there won't be any homework, right?

THE END

Surely you can find somebody who's in charge — or at least somebody who speaks English. You set off down the corridor, keeping an eye out for any other people.

It doesn't take long. After you've walked for maybe a minute, a big door to your right slides open. More people in silver and white jumpsuits run out, just as panicked as that first guy.

'Excuse me!' you say, trying to get someone's attention. 'Excuse me! Does anyone here speak English? Can anybody help me?'

One woman points a finger back towards the room and says something in that weird language again. Then she runs off.

You look past her into the room. It just looks like a big, empty, round room, but you can't see all of it. Maybe there's someone else in there. You walk in, looking around cautiously.

GO ON TO THE NEXT PAGE.

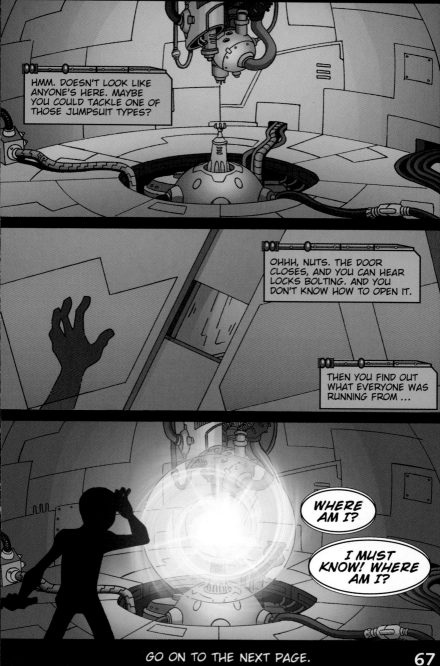

You're trapped in here . . . and that voice is loud and scary . . . but at least it's in a language you understand.

WILL YOU SAY . . .

. . . 'How am I supposed to know where you are? I don't know where I am'?

TURN TO PAGE 9.

. . . 'I don't know where you are. I just got here myself'?

TURN TO PAGE 23.

. . . 'You've got to help me! I got zapped here by a time machine'?

TURN TO PAGE 30.

'There's a lot more of you than him!' you tell the small crowd. 'Get rid of him! Tie him up or something!'

'That's true,' someone whispers. The murmuring grows.

The caveman shouts, 'Quiet! You be quiet!' and draws back his club to swing at you . . .

. . . but three of the men rush him. Suddenly everybody piles on top of the caveman. 'Hold him down!' someone screams. 'Get his club!'

Two minutes later, the caveman sits on the ground, bound hand and foot with strong vines. 'I get you!' he growls. 'I break vines and kill you all!'

'Not a chance,' you say. 'We are leaving.' The crowd follows you through the doorway . . .

. . . and you're back at the science competition! You're getting plenty of weird looks too. 'I know it's not your home,' you tell the travellers. 'But I think you'll find there's less chance of getting eaten here!'

THE END

You stay perfectly still, watching the dinosaur.

It gets even closer to the doorway. Through the portal, you can hear the sounds of the science competition. You can even make out the headmaster's voice, telling everyone to evacuate. Sounds as if Jimmy's machine is still causing trouble.

You don't dare shout a warning.

The dinosaur's nose touches the doorway — and it roars as it starts to get pulled in! The sound is so loud, it's painful, as the huge, savage creature disappears through the doorway, little by little, until it's all gone.

And the doorway disappears.

It's then that you realize something. *Wait a minute. How am I going to get back?*

You're stuck here now — wherever 'here' is.

One of those birds wheels by overhead again. It's awfully big and . . . whoa. That bird has teeth.

Welcome to your new home!

THE END

71

You don't understand what's going on, but if that guy in the jumpsuit thought it was so important, maybe you should at least look through the door. There might be somebody through there that speaks English, anyway.

You open the door. Inside is a very small room with a chair and a computer console. On the screen are four lines of text. One reads, 'HELP IN ENGLISH.'

All right! You sit down in the chair — and the door seals shut behind you.

Why didn't I see that coming? you think.

There's no keyboard. To the computer, you say, 'Uh . . . I speak English.'

The screen changes. Now it's a map of the world below, with three glowing red dots. They're labelled London, Mexico City and Antarctica.

And then suddenly you're moving! A computerized voice says, 'Escape pod launch successful.'

You just got shot out of the space station!

GO ON TO THE NEXT PAGE.

The computer voice says,
'Choose destination from highlighted selections.'

WILL YOU CHOOSE . . .

. . . London?

TURN TO PAGE 26.

. . . Antarctica?

TURN TO PAGE 87.

. . . Mexico City?

TURN TO PAGE 109.

YOU'VE READ A LITTLE BIT ABOUT ANTARCTICA, AND YOU THINK THIS IS PROBABLY AS WARM AS IT'S GOING TO GET.

YOU'D BETTER GET MOVING BEFORE YOU END UP AN ICICLE.

WELL ... THIS IS EAST ... SO THAT'S GOT TO BE THE US BASE.

BETTER GO SAY HELLO!

GO ON TO THE NEXT PAGE.

You make your way down the slope and go to the biggest building. You notice how there's no snow on the roofs or the walls. That must mean the heat's on inside, right?

The big main door isn't locked. You swing it open and look inside. All the lights are off except for a couple of small red ones. 'Hello?' You're afraid to speak too loudly.

This place is creepy.

It is indeed warm inside, so you step in. The door swings shut behind you. 'Anybody here?'

Suddenly there's a buzzing sound. You look up and see a speaker mounted on the wall — the kind that's part of a PA system. A voice comes from the speaker . . .

'You! You are . . . human?'

There's something weird about that voice. Something not natural. Like it's from a computer, maybe?

GO ON TO THE NEXT PAGE.

'Uh . . . yeah . . . I'm human.'

'Please come to the conference room at the end of the hall,' the voice says.

You don't like the way the voice sounds. But you can't think of anything else to do. Slowly, carefully, you move down the hallway to the conference room.

Suddenly you're pulled inside!

Standing there staring at you with glowing yellow eyes are three robots. Even though they're machines, you can tell, they hate you.

'Finally,' one says. 'We scared the humans off their precious space station. Our plan worked! The escape pods cooperated!'

'Wh-wh-what's going on?' you stammer.

'What's going on,' another robot says, 'is that we're now one child closer to eliminating all humans!' It sprays you in the face with some kind of gas.

Things get dark very quickly. And you're pretty sure you're not going to wake up.

THE END

You have no idea what's happening here.

WILL YOU . . .

. . . try to explore the station and
work out what's what?
TURN TO PAGE 66.

. . . follow the strange man's advice
and go through the door?
TURN TO PAGE 72.

GO ON TO THE NEXT PAGE.

There in front of you is the Russian research base. It's got a huge bio-dome-type structure built onto one side of it, like a huge glass bowl turned upside down. And inside that dome, it looks as if it could be summer! Trees blossom, flowers grow . . . and as you get closer, you see a group of men and women having a barbecue!

They spot you and motion for you to come inside.

'How did you get here?' one of the women asks you once you enter the dome. Between bites of sausage sandwich (you were really hungry!), you tell her about the time travel machine and the accident and all the crazy stuff you've been through.

'Time travel?' says one of the men. Everyone stops and looks at you. A murmur goes through the crowd. 'Time travel?' 'Accident?'

'Here,' the woman says, taking your arm. 'You should come with me.'

GO ON TO THE NEXT PAGE.

Bewildered, you follow the woman inside the base, out of the bio-dome. She takes you down a short hallway and opens a door at the end. 'Take a look,' she says.

Inside the room is a very sophisticated-looking machine. Suddenly you realize that it's like a grown-up version of Jimmy's machine!

'What is this thing?' you ask the woman.

'It's our time machine,' she says. 'Latest model: the Noseleather 6000.'

You can't believe it. Looks as if Jimmy probably won that science competition!

'Would you like us to send you back to your own time?' she asks politely.

You start laughing in spite of yourself. 'Yeah,' you tell her. 'Yeah, I would. But . . . do you think I could have another sausage sandwich first?'

THE END

No point in not being honest now. While the wizard listens attentively, you explain everything — the future, the science competition, Jimmy Noseleather, all of it.

When you're done, the wizard hoots and grins and claps his hands together. 'I knew it! I knew time travel was possible! I've been working on it myself!' He's practically dancing. 'I could tell from the moment I saw you that you were different! This is fantastic!'

A familiar voice reaches you. 'What's different? What is happening?' You turn and see Princess Genevieve emerge from a secret panel on one side of the room.

'I thought you were a prisoner!' you exclaim.

'I am,' she says. 'I cannot leave the castle. But within the castle, I roam free. I have been helping the wizard when I can. I am his assistant, you see.'

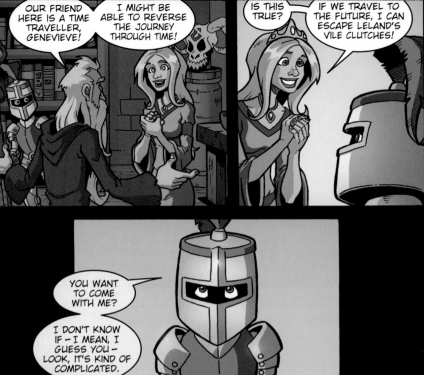

These two have been really nice to you. But how could they possibly fit into the modern world?

WILL YOU...

...rush through the doorway alone?
TURN TO PAGE 21.

...agree to take the princess with you?
TURN TO PAGE 25.

...invite them to come to the future with you?
TURN TO PAGE 105.

...explain how you have to leave them behind?
TURN TO PAGE 71.

These people are way too far gone for you to try to help. The only option is to jump through the doorway by yourself and hope it takes you back home.

But the caveman seems to know what you're planning even before you do it. You try to duck and dash away from him, but his hand clamps down on the back of your neck.

'I say you stay here!' His breath in your face is awful.

'No!' you shout. 'I won't be one of your . . . your . . . whatever these people are! I won't do it!'

His eyes narrow. 'You tell truth. You not ever gonna do what I say.'

'Right! Now you're getting it.'

'Fine,' he says – and then he flings you completely off the terrace, out into the air.

As you're falling towards the valley floor, so very far below, a thought occurs to you. Maybe staying there and being the caveman's pet human wouldn't have been that bad . . .

THE END

85

'Look, there's been a huge misunderstanding,' you call out, edging your horse towards the doorway. 'I don't want to fight.'

Everyone stops what they're doing and stares at you. Everyone except Sir Hogarth the Vicious, that is. He nudges his horse and starts moving towards you.

Maybe it'll help if you take off your helmet. 'Hang on a second,' you shout. 'I don't want to fight! Look, I'm not who you think I am!'

The helmet won't come off . . . and Sir Hogarth is speeding up! You look around for the squire, but he's van- ished. 'Wait, wait, wait!' you cry out.

Sir Hogarth is galloping now. 'Death to all cowards!' he screams. You see the point of his lance coming right at you. Your horse won't budge, and you can barely move in the armour. . . and just before the impact, you realize that for you, this is

THE END

You heave the canister at the doorway plants.

It goes off like a gas bomb! Immediately the plants start to turn yellow and die! You pour on a burst of speed and fling yourself through the doorway . . .

. . . but you feel something wrap around your ankle as you're going through.

Immediately you're back at the science competition, right next to Jimmy Noseleather's table. But the doorway is still open, and there's a huge tendril coming through it. As you watch, more and more tendrils poke through the doorway.

'Turn off the machine, Jimmy!' you scream.

Jimmy yells, 'I don't know how!'

You scramble up and do the only thing you can think of. You throw the machine through the doorway!

There's an explosion . . . and then the doorway and the plants are gone. 'My machine!' Jimmy wails. 'You destroyed my machine!'

Somehow, you just can't feel too guilty about that.

THE END

89

TURN TO PAGE 8.

As the lawman starts to stand up, you fall flat on your belly. Your pistol skids away under a chair and you put your hands on your head.

It's a good thing, too, that you got out of the way. The lawman roars, 'Reach for the sky, you villains!' A second later, the car is filled with deafening gunfire.

Then the lawman squats down next to you. He seems to be just fine. You don't think you could say the same for the rest of the outlaws.

'Get up, you yellow-bellied varmint!' he says and prods you with this gun. 'You may've been smart enough not to get shot, but you ain't smart enough not to go to jail!'

On the floor or not, he still thinks you're part of the gang!

GO ON TO THE NEXT PAGE.

You've got to tell this guy something before
he drags you away to prison!

WILL YOU SAY . . .

. . . 'Don't shoot!
I'm from the future!'
TURN TO PAGE 89.

. . . 'Don't shoot!
I'm only a kid!'
TURN TO PAGE 50.

The baron brings you and Genevieve into a beautiful, ornate room. He takes a seat on a big, heavy wooden chair and makes you stand before him. Then the blacksmith arrives to pry the helmet off your head. It's good to breathe fresh air again!

The baron scowls at you. 'What? You are but a child! How came you to be here?'

'Well, my lord,' you begin, 'I'm actually from the future. You see, there was a machine at this place, and it didn't work properly, and this doorway opened up and . . .'

You trail off. The baron isn't understanding a single word coming out of your mouth.

'Guards!' he shouts. 'Methinks this youth is a witch! Cast the witch into the dungeon, so that no more evil may plague us!'

GO ON TO THE NEXT PAGE.

That doorway is your first priority. You run towards it, but the baron grabs you! 'You'll not escape me!' he snarls.

Then he sees the doorway too. 'What is this black magic? Answer me!' You don't pay any attention to him. You just keep running, dragging him along, and suddenly you're both back at the science fair!

Baron Leland waves his sword around. 'What sort of sorcery is this? What is this place? Someone answer me, or I start cutting off heads!'

Well, that does the trick. You hear someone dial 999, and a few minutes later, the police arrive. Baron Leland gets hit with pepper spray and carted off in hand-cuffs.

'Now,' a detective says to you, 'mind explaining who that fellow is — and exactly what you're doing in a suit of armour?'

'I'll tell you the whole story,' you say, 'if you'll just get me out of this thing!'

THE END

There's no time to lose. You race into the sea as fast as you can. It gets deep pretty quickly and in a few seconds, you're far enough out that you're treading water.

It worked! The dinosaur has stopped right at the water-line. It just stands there glaring at you.

Then you see something out of the corner of your eye. Something just moved in the water off to your right. Something big.

But that's not the only thing that catches your attention.

Behind you, maybe ten or fifteen feet under the water, is a doorway! It's just like the one you came through. If you can get to it, it might take you home!

You can tell the next few seconds
will mean life or death.

WILL YOU...

...put some distance between you
and whatever that big thing is?

TURN TO PAGE 81.

...dive under and try to make it to
the doorway, even though you don't
know what else is down there?

TURN TO PAGE 10.

THE DINOSAUR ISN'T GROWLING OR ROARING, BUT YOU KNOW IT'S RIGHT BEHIND YOU. YOU CAN HEAR ITS FOOTSTEPS GETTING CLOSER.

ALMOST THERE! JUST A LITTLE FURTHER AND YOU CAN JUMP IN THE WATER. MAYBE, IF YOU'RE REALLY LUCKY, THE DINOSAUR WON'T FOLLOW YOU IN THERE.

THEN YOU TRIP. OH, NO!

BUT THE DINOSAUR HASN'T POUNCED ON YOU QUITE YET...

98

TURN TO PAGE 40.

Slowly you raise your pistol and level it at the lawman. 'N-n-now, don't do anything foolish, mister!'

The other outlaws hear you and spin around. 'Lookee here, boys! We got us a hero! Let's fill 'im full o' lead!'

Then the lawman moves. You've never seen anybody this fast in your life. He stands up, draws his gun, and slaps your pistol aside. You stumble backwards and crack your head on something, and just as you're losing consciousness, you hear a roar of gunfire.

When you wake up, you're in a different car — and you're chained to the seat! The lawman sits across from you. 'Real shame,' he says, 'when a child as young as you goes so wrong. Ah, well. Nothin' a few years of hard labour won't fix. You'll prob'ly get released when you're twenty, twenty-five, or so.'

Twenty-five? Well ... it's not all bad. You'll definitely get plenty of exercise!

THE END

You saw a movie once where this worked. Hoping against hope, you stay exactly where you are. You don't move. You don't breathe.

The dinosaur stops . . . looks around . . . blinks its eyes . . . Could this be working?

Then the huge creature cocks its head to one side and sniffs.

That's it, you think. *I'm dead.*

But then, right before your eyes, a doorway appears! It's right between you and the dinosaur.

The creature blinks again, pauses for a second, and then moves closer to the doorway. It seems to be fascinated by it.

The dinosaur gets closer and closer to the doorway, and you think it might have forgotten about you.

GO ON TO THE NEXT PAGE.

You're in an awfully tight spot.

WILL YOU...

... stay where you are and hope the doorway will pull the dinosaur through it, just like it did to you?

TURN TO PAGE 70.

... try to make it through the doorway, even though it means getting closer to the dinosaur?

TURN TO PAGE 11.

TURN TO PAGE 77.

These guys look pretty dangerous. You'd better play along with them for now, or they might just shoot you and leave you out here in the desert. Besides, there could be somebody on the train who can help.

You scramble up onto your horse. When the train gets closer, you ride along with the rest of the outlaws. One by one, they jump onto the train, standing on the little balcony outside the caboose. The last guy reaches out, grabs your arm and hauls you up with the rest of them.

'This ain't nothin' fancy,' one of them says. 'Just like we planned it. Go in, take their money, blow the safe and get back off. Everybody clear?'

You nod, but you're thinking of an escape. Maybe you could just jump back off. But the train's moving awfully fast, and what if you broke a leg when you landed? Better follow the outlaws in.

TURN TO PAGE 111.

'This should take me back to my own time,' you tell them. 'Would the two of you like to come with me?'

Both the wizard and the princess eagerly accept your invitation. You step through together and find yourselves right outside the school, with the science competition still going on.

'This is it,' you tell them. 'This is where I came from. Are you sure you'll be okay here?'

'Oh, I think we'll manage,' the wizard tells you. They both thank you sincerely and then the wizard gestures. They both vanish in a flash of light. Great – now all you have to do is get this armour off.

Two weeks later, you see an article in the newspaper: NEW MAGIC ACT BECOMES THE TOAST OF LONDON. You recognize the wizard, even in his tuxedo, and the princess as his onstage assistant. Looks as if they're managing just fine!

THE END

Before you know it, you're through the doorway. You find yourself standing on the side of a rocky hill, surrounded by weird vegetation. It looks as if it's just rained. There are lots of little puddles around.

To your right, over the top of the hill, you spot a thin wisp of smoke rising up. You think it might be from a campfire.

To your left, the hill slopes sharply down. Maybe a hundred yards away, there's a narrow beach . . . and then what looks like an ocean.

A big bird you don't recognize flies overhead and lets out a harsh, ugly call.

What happened? Where are you?

GO ON TO THE NEXT PAGE.

You've got to run!

WILL YOU...

... head towards the ocean, since you'll move a lot faster going downhill?

TURN TO PAGE 98.

... run up and over the hill, towards the campfire smoke?

TURN TO PAGE 42.

You've made your choice — Mexico City. As the pod descends, the computer gives you a jumpsuit, a helmet, and a canister of chemicals. You ask what it is, but the computer won't say anything except 'herbicide.' Herbicide? Like what your dad sprays on weeds? Huh. All right.

You wriggle into the jumpsuit and pull on the helmet. Minutes later, the pod lands with a thump. Cautiously you ask, 'So . . . what's it like out there?'

'Readings inconclusive,' the computer says. OK. What the heck does that mean?

You look outside. Your eyes get huge.

You know you're in the future, but you're pretty sure Mexico City isn't supposed to look like this.

There are plants. Plants everywhere! The whole city has been overrun with plants. Huge, thick, greenish blue vines that cover entire buildings and burst through the pavement of the streets. How did this happen? Was it some kind of experiment that went horribly wrong?

TURN TO PAGE 104.

You can't believe the nerve of this guy! And why is everybody else just standing around looking scared?

'I don't take kindly to threats,' you say, giving the caveman your best 'tough' look.

You hear a tiny voice from the crowd: 'Don't make him angry!'

But it's too late for that. 'You do what I say!' he shouts. 'Everybody do what I say! I'm biggest! I'm in charge!'

'You don't scare me, you big jerk! Now, are you all going to help me work out how to get out of here? Or are you just going to stand around and look stupid?'

Then you notice that the caveman has drawn back the huge club he's carrying. You realize you might have been a tad too forceful in an unfamiliar situation. Before you can move, the club crashes down on your head and for you this is most definitely

THE END

WHICH TWISTED JOURNEYS® WILL YOU TRY NEXT?

#1 CAPTURED BY PIRATES
Can you keep a band of scurvy pirates from turning you into shark bait?

#2 ESCAPE FROM PYRAMID X
Not every ancient mummy stays dead . . .

#3 TERROR IN GHOST MANSION
The spooks in this Halloween house aren't wearing costumes . . .

#4 THE TREASURE OF MOUNT FATE
Can you survive monsters and magic and bring home the treasure?

#5 NIGHTMARE ON ZOMBIE ISLAND
Will you be the first to escape Zombie Island?

#6 THE TIME TRAVEL TRAP
Danger is everywhere when you're caught in a time machine!

#7 VAMPIRE HUNT
Vampire hunters are creeping through an ancient castle. And they're hunting you.

#8 ALIEN INCIDENT ON PLANET J
Make peace with the Makaknuk, Zirifubi and Frongo, or you'll never get off their planet . . .

#9 AGENT MONGOOSE AND THE HYPNO-BEAM SCHEME
Your top-secret mission, if you choose to accept it: foil the plots of an evil mastermind!

#10 THE GOBLIN KING
Will you join the fearsome goblins or the dangerous elves?